Mimi's Birthday Trip

Contents

Written by Tom Ottway

Illustrated by Adrienn Greta Schönberg

Collins

What's in this story?

Listen and say

superhero

cinema

money

ticket

space

scary

popcorn

bottle of water

This story is about my sister, Mimi, and her birthday trip to the cinema. I love my sister and I was very happy when Mum and Dad said, "You and Calvin can take Mimi to the cinema." Calvin is my best friend.

Me (Jake)

Calvin

But the bad **news** was ... we also took Mimi's six friends: Adra and Pritti, Dizzie, Freddy, Sam and Sid.

It's my birthday!

Mimi

Adra

Pritti

Dizzie

Freddy

Sam

Sid

My sister, Mimi, is seven years old. Sometimes she's really nice, but sometimes she's a little bit difficult.

Sometimes she's happy ...

... but then she cries!

Then she's happy again!

My best friend Calvin is very nice.
He doesn't talk a lot, but he smiles all the time.
He likes taking photos and video on his phone.
He's very good at making films.

Smile!

Chapter 2 At the cinema

Calvin and I took Mimi and her friends to the cinema. It was a hot, sunny day. We walked from our house, **near** the park, then we all took the bus to the cinema.

It wasn't easy. They didn't listen.

Come on, everyone!

At the cinema, Adra and Pritti needed to go to the bathroom. We waited and waited and waited ...

Then everyone said, "We're hungry."

Mimi said very loudly, "Who wants **popcorn**?"

"Yes, please!" they all said.

"Please, Jake!" said Mimi. "It's my birthday!"

"Oh, OK," I said.

So I waited a long time for popcorn and I paid a lot of **money** for it.

There were lots of good films at the cinema. Which film was best? It was difficult. Mimi's friends didn't want to see the **same** film!

"Listen!" I said. "What about *Bee Quick*?"

"What's it about?" asked Mimi.

"It's about a very fast bee," I said.

"There's **Space** *Sharks*," I said. "It's a film about a shark who goes to space."

"**Maybe**," said Mimi.

"Yes, please!" said Freddy. "I love animals."

"But it's very long," said Sid. "I can't sit for two hours!"

"Oh yes, it finishes **late**. We can't watch that," I said.

"Look, there's a **superhero** film!" I said.
"It's about a girl and a boy who grow and
shrink. They can be very small or very big."

"Yes, please!" said Dizzie. "That's **cool**!"

uick

Then Mimi said, "I know. Let's not see *that* film. Let's see *Bonzo's Breakfast*. It's a funny film. Look!"

"Yes!" said everyone.

"Do you all **agree**?" I asked. "Is everyone happy?"

18

"Yes!" said everyone.

Mimi's friends all agreed, so I bought nine tickets for *Bonzo's Breakfast*.

Bonzo's Breakfast

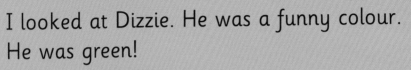

I looked at Dizzie. He was a funny colour.
He was green!

"I don't **feel well**," said Dizzie.

"He ate all my popcorn!" said Freddy.

"He ate mine, too," said Sam.

I got some water for Dizzie.

"Can I have some water, please?" said Adra and Pritti.

I bought three bottles of water.

Dizzie drank all his water. Then, after two or three minutes, he wasn't green.

"Good!" I said to Calvin.

Calvin smiled.

Chapter 3 The film

I gave the man our tickets. It was **dark** in the cinema. Sid knew a lot about the film. He said, "Do you know it only took three weeks to make this film? That's very quick."

"Wait," said Freddy. "I saw this film last week!"

"What?" I said. "You didn't say that when I bought the tickets!"

Calvin smiled.

Oh no! Mimi is crying. This is not good.
This is bad ...

"It's not a **scary** film, Mimi!" said Freddy.
"Wait and see!"

Bonzo's Breakfast

I don't like this!

"Sorry … Let's go, everyone!" I said to Mimi's friends.

"But I like it," said Pritti.

"Me too!" said Adra.

"I didn't finish my popcorn!" said Sid.

"Sorry, Sid," I said. "It *is* Mimi's birthday."

Chapter 4 Jake and Calvin's fantastic idea

Calvin and I took Mimi and her friends home. They had food and drinks and played games. Mimi liked her birthday cake, but she was sad about the cinema trip.

Calvin and I looked at the photos and video on Calvin's phone. And then we had a fantastic idea ...

"Let's watch a film!" I said.

Yes, please!

27

Calvin and I made a film on my computer. It was very funny. I think everyone liked it!

Happy birthday, Mimi!

Thank you! This isn't scary!

"You've got a nice brother," said Adra.

"And he's got a cool friend," said Dizzie.

"We can go to the cinema again tomorrow," said Pritti.

Mimi smiled. "Maybe not," she said.

Mini-dictionary

Listen and read

agree (verb) If people **agree**, they think the same as each other about something.

cool (adjective) If you think that something is **cool**, you think it is interesting or exciting.

dark (adjective) A **dark** place has very little light in it, or no light at all.

feel well (phrasal verb) If you don't **feel well**, you are ill.

late (adverb) If something finishes **late**, it finishes near the end of the day.

maybe (adverb) You say **maybe** when you are not sure about something.

money (noun) **Money** is the coins or notes that you use to buy things.

near (preposition) If something is **near** a place, it is not very far away from it.

news (noun) If someone tells you bad **news**, they tell you something that makes you sad.

popcorn (noun) **Popcorn** is grains of corn that you cook and they become large and light.

same (adjective) If you are talking about the **same** thing, you are talking about only one thing, and not different ones.

scary (adjective) Something that is **scary** makes you feel afraid.

shrink (verb) If someone or something **shrinks**, they become smaller in size.

space (noun) **Space** is the area above the Earth, where the stars and planets are.

superhero (noun) A **superhero** is someone in a film or a book who is able to do special things to help others.

1 Look and order the story

2 Listen and say

Collins

Published by Collins
An imprint of HarperCollins*Publishers*
Westerhill Road
Bishopbriggs
Glasgow
G64 2QT

HarperCollins*Publishers*
1st Floor, Watermarque Building
Ringsend Road
Dublin 4
Ireland

William Collins' dream of knowledge for all began with the publication of his first book in 1819.

A self-educated mill worker, he not only enriched millions of lives, but also founded a flourishing publishing house. Today, staying true to this spirit, Collins books are packed with inspiration, innovation and practical expertise. They place you at the centre of a world of possibility and give you exactly what you need to explore it.

ISBN 978-0-00-839741-8

Collins® and COBUILD® are registered trademarks of HarperCollins*Publishers* Limited

www.collins.co.uk/elt

British Library Cataloguing in Publication Data

A catalogue record for this publication is available from the British Library.

Author: Tom Ottway
Illustrator: Adrienn Greta Schönberg (Beehive)
Series editor: Rebecca Adlard
Publishing manager: Lisa Todd
Product managers: Jennifer Hall and Caroline Green
In-house editor: Alma Puts Keren
Project manager: Emily Hooton
Editor: Matthew Hancock
Proofreaders: Natalie Murray and Michael Lamb
Cover designer: Kevin Robbins
Typesetter: 2Hoots Publishing Services Ltd
Audio produced by id audio, London
Reading guide author: Emma Wilkinson
Production controller: Rachel Weaver
Printed and bound by: GPS Group, Slovenia

Download the audio for this book and a reading guide for parents and teachers at www.collins.co.uk/839741